Carrie's Gift

EFNER TUDOR HOLMES

Illustrated by TASHA TUDOR

COLLINS + WORLD

New York and Cleveland

Library of Congress Cataloging in Publication Data

Holmes, Efner Tudor. Carrie's gift.

SUMMARY: Carrie's attempts to befriend the
dour old man on the neighboring farm are resisted
until they save her dog from a trap together.
[1. Friendship—Fiction. 2. Country life—Fic-
tion]
I. Tudor, Tasha. II. Title.
PZ7.H735Car   [Fic]   78-8452
                ISBN 0-529-05428-0
                ISBN 0-529-05429-9 lib. bdg.

Published by William Collins + World Publishing Company,
New York and Cleveland, 1978.

Carrie's Gift

Ever since Carrie could remember, Old Duncan had lived in the house that lay across the big field from her family's farm, yet she had never met him or spoken to him. He lived alone in the little house covered with honeysuckle and vines.

Sometimes Carrie and her brothers would lie on their stomachs behind the wall that separated the two homes, to try and catch a glimpse of the old man. But they seldom saw him. His house stood in silence, with an air of mysterious solitude.

In summer the grass in his yard grew to the windowsills. Any gardens that once might have graced the house had long since grown to orchard grass.

It was said that Old Duncan had no human friends. But many times people had seen deer nibbling at the old apple trees that grew in his yard, their gnarled branches bent low to the ground. And a raccoon lived in the big maple tree; she came every evening for her saucer of bread and milk. If they had been able to look more closely, they would have known there was a woodchuck, too, who brought her family to romp in the grass as Duncan sat on his granite step smoking his pipe. Duncan talked to all of the forest creatures as if he were one of them.

Now, as Carrie stood in the sun-flecked wood, her hand resting on the head of her dog, Heidi, she suddenly saw the old man. Unaware of her presence, he sat on a rock beside the brook that rushed past him, tumbling into rocky pools. In his hands he had a dry twig, which he was slowly breaking. One by one, he threw the bits of wood into the water, watching them disappear, twisting in the strong current. He looked so alone that Carrie was suddenly tempted to go and talk to him.

Just then Duncan stood up. Heidi rushed forward,

barking. Surprised, the old man bent down and held out his hand to the dog. As he did, he saw Carrie.

"Call off your dog," he said.

"She won't hurt you," said Carrie. "See, she likes you."

"Well, I don't have any use for people who spy on others," Duncan said.

He turned and walked into the woods. Carrie stared after him for a moment, stung by his unpleasantness. Then she started back toward home, Heidi running ahead. It was only when she came to a sandy clearing where she found a patch of wild strawberries that her spirits lifted. She stopped to pick some, filling her mouth with their sun-warmed sweetness. Her thoughts strayed back to the old man, with his guarded solitude.

The next morning, even though it was early, the heat lay over the farm in breathless stillness. Carrie returned to the clearing to pick more berries. She liked picking; the sun felt pleasantly hot on her back, and the deep silence of the woods was broken only by the birds calling.

A voice made her jump. There stood Old Duncan, watching her, two buckets of berries tied to his belt.

"If it's good berries you want, there's a better patch than this. Go to the brook, beyond where you were yesterday. There's another clearing up ahead."

He turned abruptly toward his home.

"Wait," called Carrie. "Wouldn't you come with me?"

The old man turned and looked back at the girl as she stood waiting. He hesitated a moment; then he pulled his cap down hard over his eyes, hiding the surprised pleasure that flickered over his face.

"You'll find them all right," he replied. He walked away, the buckets of berries bumping against his legs.

Early that same evening, Carrie walked across the field toward Duncan's house. She carried a plate of strawberry shortcake, wrapped in a napkin. Though she walked at a brisk pace, her heart pounded in nervous hesitation. When she came to the stone wall, she crouched down to peer cautiously over the top. Old Duncan was nowhere in sight. The house, shaded in vines and trees, was enveloped in

silence. Yet as Carrie watched, she saw that the yard was full of life. Rabbits were nibbling at the grass; swallows flew back and forth to their nests under the eaves; and Carrie was fascinated to see two deer eating the leaves from a clump of lilacs banking the house.

She straightened up and slipped over the low wall. Then she walked slowly through the high grass toward the wide granite step. It was still daylight, and she wondered if she were being watched. Reaching the step, she set the plate down and turned to go.

An animal's cry, full of pain and terror, cut into the peaceful silence. The other animals scattered in alarm and vanished.

Carrie stood still, a sudden premonition filling her with dread. The cry sounded like that of a dog. Heidi had been

gone all afternoon. Heidi! Carrie began to run into the
woods, calling her dog's name, unaware of the sound of
footsteps behind her.

She found Heidi, her front leg caught in the sharp teeth
of a steel trap. When the dog saw her, she was quiet for an
instant, looking at Carrie with eyes darkened in pain. Then

she renewed her frenzied cries and began biting at her leg,
trying to pull it free.

Carrie tried to hold the dog still so she could spring the
trap, but Heidi, frantic, no longer herself, snapped at her
viciously. Carrie jumped back, then stood for a moment,
clenching her hands in despair as she realized she could not

save Heidi by herself. Then she turned and started to run toward Duncan's house. But the old man was running to meet her.

"Quick, girl, what is it?" he asked.

"It's Heidi, my dog," Carrie cried. "She's in a trap, and I can't get her out. Oh, please help."

They came to Heidi, now lying still but whimpering.

"She's going into shock," said Duncan. "Hold her tight, though."

In one quick motion he loosened the jaws of the trap. Carrie gasped when she saw the injured paw. Without a word, Duncan picked up the dog. Carrie ran ahead, holding branches back, clearing the way.

In his house Old Duncan put Heidi gently down on a wooden table in the middle of the low-ceilinged kitchen.

"Heat some water," he said to Carrie. Then he went outside, returning presently with bunches of healing herbs and leaves in his hand.

"I'd like to get my hands on the fellow who set that trap!" he said vehemently. "And on my land, too!"

He looked at Carrie, and his face softened. The girl looked drained, her face pale against her dark hair.

"She'll walk again," he said gruffly.

Moonlight was spilling through the kitchen windows
when Duncan straightened up from the table.

"She must stay here tonight—maybe longer," he said.
"I have to change the dressings and keep an eye on her."

Carrie looked at him gratefully. "Thank you," she said.

"And I'd better go home now. But I'll be back tomorrow."

Duncan didn't answer, and she felt suddenly awkward. The old man was watching her, but not unkindly. On impulse, she reached up and kissed him on the cheek. Then she stepped into the fragrant night.

Old Duncan stood in the doorway watching her
disappear through the tall grass. Something white caught his
eye and, looking down, he saw the gift Carrie had left—the

strawberry shortcake, neatly wrapped in its napkin. He
smiled and bent down to pick it up.

The shortcake eaten, Old Duncan looked inside the

kitchen, where Heidi now lay sleeping quietly. For a long
time after that, he sat in the moonlight, the empty plate in his
lap, his hand touching his cheek.